UNCLE MELVIN

UNCLE MELVIN

DANIEL PINKWATER

Macmillan Publishing Company   New York

Macmillan Publishing Company
866 Third Avenue, New York, NY 10022
Collier Macmillan Canada, Inc.
Printed and bound in Singapore   First American Edition

10 9 8 7 6 5 4 3 2 1

The text of this book is set in 14 point Stempel Schneidler.
The illustrations are rendered in pen-and-ink with color markers.

Library of Congress Cataloging-in-Publication Data
Pinkwater, Daniel Manus, date. Uncle Melvin.
Summary: Charles enjoys spending time with his gentle Uncle Melvin,
even though Melvin harbors strange delusions about his own power
to talk to the birds or control the rain.
[1. Mentally ill—Fiction. 2. Uncles—Fiction] I. Title.
PZ7.P6335Un   1989   [E]   88-27178
ISBN 0-02-774675-5

For Jill,

who points out rainbows

My uncle Melvin comes to my house every day. At night he goes back to the Looney Bin. He calls it the Looney Bin. It's a special place for crazy people. Uncle Melvin lives there because he's crazy.

My parents leave for work early in the morning. Uncle Melvin makes my breakfast and walks me to school. Then he goes home and takes care of the house. He cleans up, and does a lot of stuff in the garden.

When school is over, Uncle Melvin is waiting for me. He walks me home and stays until my parents get back and it's time for him to go to the Looney Bin.

"Hello, Melvin. Hello, Charles," my mother says. "Did you have a good day?"

"The dog is mad at me," Uncle Melvin might say. "She isn't speaking to me, but she'll get over it."

Sometimes Melvin does strange things because he's crazy. For example, one morning he made me a fried-egg sandwich for breakfast. This sandwich had a slice of toast between two fried eggs.

Another time he mowed the lawn, but he left a big X unmowed in the middle. Then he collected a lot of stones and painted them white. He arranged the stones to spell out

FLYING SAUCERS!
LAND HERE!
PLEASE! I AM YOUR FRIEND.

Uncle Melvin talks to himself. He also talks to me. He talks to me when we are walking to school and when we walk back. He tells me about his theories. One of his theories is that the President of the United States is an iguana—that's a big lizard. He says the President wears a President mask and a President suit, but underneath he's an iguana.

Uncle Melvin says he can talk to birds and animals. He says they can talk to him and he understands what they are saying.

"See that young cat?" Melvin asks me. "He's the playboy of the Western world. He doesn't know there's anything he can't defeat. He's handsome, strong, and stupid as the sky is blue. He won't listen to me."

The birds really do seem to listen to Melvin. Whenever he goes outside, the birds all start to whistle and chirp, and Uncle Melvin whistles back to them.

I asked my father, "Can Uncle Melvin really understand what the birds are saying?"

"Maybe he can," my father said. "When we were boys, wild birds would perch on his fingers."

"Maybe sometime I'll teach you to talk to the birds," Uncle Melvin says.

Uncle Melvin got an old-fashioned hat. It's a derby—one of those round hats. He wears it all the time. It looks strange with his blue jeans and green suspenders.

"This hat gives me power," he says. "The round shape of the inside of the hat causes my thoughts to bounce back into my brain. That way they can't get away until I'm finished with them."

Uncle Melvin told me he was noticing something strange.

"What I'm noticing," he said, "is that I seem to be able to control when it rains and when it stops."

"You can control when it rains and when it stops?"

"No matter how hard it's raining," Uncle Melvin said, "when I go outside, it stops. Then I noticed that if I turn to the left, fast—it starts raining again. If I turn to the right, I get a rainbow."

"Really?"

"Really."

I talked to my father. "Uncle Melvin says he can cause it to rain and to stop raining. Is that possible?"

"No," my father said. "It is not possible."

"He says he can make a rainbow."

"Uncle Melvin is a special person," my father said. "He sees the world in his own way. But he cannot make it rain or make it stop raining or cause a rainbow."

"You said he could understand the birds."

"I said maybe," my father said. "I said maybe he could understand the birds—in a way—in his own way. I do not believe he can talk with them the way you and I are talking now."

"Oh."

"I don't want you to argue with Melvin—and I know you won't make fun of him."

"You mean because he's crazy?"

"Charles, I have never thought of Melvin as crazy. In many ways he is the least crazy person I know. He has his ideas—that's all."

"My father doesn't believe you can do that stuff with the rain," I said to Uncle Melvin.

"That's okay," Melvin said. "I wouldn't believe it myself."

On Saturdays and Sundays, Melvin spends the
whole day in the garden—unless it is covered with
snow. Then he usually hangs out in the basement,
fixing things.

One particular Saturday morning, it was raining on and off. I was in my room, putting together a model race car and listening to the radio. I happened to look out the window. Uncle Melvin was digging in the garden. There were a few birds hopping around by his feet, as usual. He was wearing his derby hat. In the sky there were four rainbows.